EVIL EMPEROR PENGUIN

LA

Evil Emperor Penguin
is a
DAVID FICKLING BOOK

First published in Great Britain in 2015 by
David Fickling Books,
31 Beaumont Street,
Oxford, OX1 2NP
www.davidficklingbooks.com

978-1-910200-51-3

1 3 5 7 9 10 8 6 4 2

David Fickling Books supports the Forest Stewardship Council (FSC), the leading international forest certification organisation. All our titles that are printed on Greenpeace-approved FSC-certified paper carry the FSC logo.

FSC www.fsc.org MIX Paper from responsible sources FSC® C020872

DAVID FICKLING BOOKS Reg. No. 8340307

A CIP catalogue record for this book is available from the British Library.

Printed and bound in Great Britain by Polestar Stones.

CONTENTS OF EVIL

EEP'S EVIL UNDERGROUND HEADQUARTERS (TOP SECRET!)

NAME: EVIL EMPEROR PENGUIN
SPECIES: PENGUIN
OCCUPATION: MEGALOMANIAC
LOVES: SPAGHETTI HOOPS
HATES: EVERYTHING ELSE
DESCRIPTION: TINY TYRANNICAL SEABIRD. ONE AIM IN LIFE... TO TAKE OVER THE WORLD!

NAME: EUGENE
SPECIES: ABOMINABLE SNOWMAN CLONE (MADE BY EEP)
OCCUPATION: TOP MINION
LOVES: EVERYTHING AND HUGS
HATES: THE THOUGHT OF NO HUGS OR NO UNICORNS
DESCRIPTION: SUPER CUDDLY WITH A PASSION FOR ALL THINGS LOVELY.

NAME: NUMBER 8
SPECIES: OCTOPUS
OCCUPATION: SIDEKICK
LOVES: KNITTING AND EUGENE
HATES: BEING CALLED 'SQUID'
DESCRIPTION: SHARPLY DRESSED AND VERY POLITE. THE CALM PURPLE 'BRAIN' OF THE GROUP.

A STITCH IN TIME

YOU MUST FOLLOW EACH INSTRUCTION *VERY* CAREFULLY, EUGENE.
WE CAN'T AFFORD FOR *ANYTHING* TO GO WRONG!
ONE MISTAKE AND YOU'RE AN ABOMINABLE PIE!

OF COURSE, EVIL MASTER. YOU'LL HAVE THE LOVELIEST EVIL INVENTION IN THE UNIVERSE!

EXCELLENT.
NUMBER 8! FETCH MY LAPTOP OF EVIL! I NEED TO CHECK MY E-VIL MAILS.

THE NEXT EVENING...
EUGENE! TIME IS UP! IS IT READY?
YES, EVIL MASTER! AND I FOLLOWED *ALL* YOUR INSTRUCTIONS.

WE WEREN'T SURE WHAT COLOURS TO HAVE SHOOT OUT OF THE EYES, BUT A FEW OF THE MINIONS AGREED ON A SELECTION THAT WOULD LOOK WONDERFUL.

AS LONG AS THE ICE LASER FREEZES WHOEVER IT SHOOTS AT, I DON'T CARE WHAT COLOUR IT IS...
BUT, SIR, I MEANT THE-
HUSH, YOU SPEAK TOO MUCH.

BEHOLD MY EVIL EMPEROR-BOT OF ICY DOOM!
THE EYES SHOOT ICY LASER BEAMS, IMMEDIATELY FREEZING ANYTHING THEY TOUCH!
ICE LASERS...?
VERY MAJESTIC, SIR.

I CAN USE THIS 'CONTROL PAD OF EVIL' TO COMMAND THE ROBOT TO MOVE AND SHOOT!
NOW, FETCH THE FLYING POD OF EVIL! TONIGHT WE *FLY!*
YAY!
THEN WE SHOULD ARRIVE IN PLENTY OF TIME FOR THE PICNIC!

THE NEXT MORNING...
EUGENE, CONFIRM LOCATION.
INSIDE THE FLYING POD OF EVIL, EVIL MASTER.
I MEANT OUR LOCATION ON THE MAP, *YOU BRAINLESS BEAN!*
OH, WE'RE APPROACHING ENGLAND...

EXCELLENT! NOW WE JUST NEED TO LOCATE 'HYDE PARK'...
DO YOU THINK THEY'LL HAVE SPAGHETTI HOOPS AT THE PICNIC, EVIL MASTER?
PAH! THOSE WORLD LEADERS AREN'T SOPHISTICATED ENOUGH TO EAT SPAGHETTI HOOPS.

THAT AFTERNOON...

THAT TERRIFYING PENGUIN ROBOT JUST KNITTED US THE BEST JUMPERS I'VE EVER SEEN!
IT'S SO SOFT!
MINE HAS ELBOW PATCHES!
OOO! I WANT ONE! SHOOT ME, OH MIGHTY JUMPER-MAKING PENGUIN-BOT!

WHAT THE...
WHAT?!
EUGENE...

PLEASE TELL ME WHY MY EVIL EMPEROR PENGUIN-BOT OF DOOM IS FIRING KNITTED JUMPERS!

I FOLLOWED THE INSTRUCTIONS WORD FOR WORD, EVIL MASTER. HONESTLY!

NUMBER 8!!! CAN YOU PLEASE FIND OUT WHY MY MINIONS ARE INCAPABLE OF CREATING ANYTHING?!
WHAT'S THE PROBLEM, SIR?

THE PROBLEM, SQUID-FACE, IS THAT MY EVIL WEAPON IS CREATING JUMPERS INSTEAD OF MASS DESTRUCTION!
I'LL INVESTIGATE, SIR...

EUGENE, I'VE SPOKEN TO NUMBER 8...
EUGENE?
WHERE'S THE CONTROL PAD OF EV-

OH MY GOSH, IT MAKES WOOLLY HATS TOO!
I HAVE TO GET ME ONE OF THOSE!

AREN'T YOU SUCH A WONDERFUL PENGUIN FOR DOING THIS!

SIR, NUMBER 8 HERE...
IT APPEARS MY WEEKLY KNITTING MAGAZINE WAS TUCKED INSIDE YOUR BOOK OF EVIL PLANS.
WHAT?!
EXPLAIN. THEY'RE GETTING AFFECTIONATE HERE...
KNITTED JUMPER
EVIL PLANS
EUGENE MAY HAVE COMBINED YOUR EVIL INSTRUCTIONS WITH THE KNITTED JUMPER INSTRUCTIONS. THIS COULD EXPLAIN THE MIX UP...

EUGENE! WE NEED TO TALK!
I KNOW WHAT'LL CHEER YOU UP, EVIL MASTER!
BEEP!

WAIT, EUGENE! NO!

THE WORLD NEWS
LOVELIEST PENGUIN IN THE WORLD MAKES BEAUTIFULLY KNITTED JUMPERS FOR DELIGHTED WORLD LEADERS.

HAVE NO FEAR

EVIL MASTER... DID YOU KNOW IT'S 'NATIONAL CROISSANT DAY' TODAY?
I DON'T CARE, EUGENE.
WOULD YOU LIKE A NATIONAL CROISSANT?
NO.

WHEN I RULE THE WORLD, I'M ABOLISHING CROISSANTS.
AND TUESDAYS.

AAAND FINISHED!
BEHOLD, MY NEWEST EVIL INVENTION!

THE FEARSOMITRON!
WITH THIS GENIUS DEVICE OF MINE, I'LL BE ABLE TO RELEASE A POWERFUL 'FEAR FOAM' UPON THE WORLD!
THIS 'FEAR FOAM' WILL MORPH INTO EVERYONE'S BIGGEST FEAR, CAUSING CHAOS AND HAVOC AMONG THE ENTIRE HUMAN RACE!
FEAR

SOON, EVERYONE ON THIS PATHETIC PLANET WILL BE HIDING AWAY FROM THEIR FEARS. I WILL BE THEIR ONLY HOPE...

THEY WILL HAVE NO CHOICE BUT TO FOLLOW MY ORDERS UNLESS THEY WANT TO LIVE A LIFE OF ULTIMATE FEAR FOREVEEEER!

FEAR!

EUGENE...I NEED YOU TO GO PRESS THE BLUE BUTTON TO PUT THE FEARSOMITRON INTO SAFETY MODE.
DO NOT, UNDER ANY CIRCUMSTANCES, PRESS THE RED BUTTON...

BLUE BUTTON PRESSED!
THIS IS JOLLY FUN.

OH WAIT... MAYBE THAT WAS THE RED BUTTON.
EUGENE, YOU BIG TOMATO! I TOLD YOU NOT TO PRESS THE RED BUTTON!
YOU'VE ACTIVATED THE FEARSOMITRON!
FEAR

I SOMETIMES FORGET THAT I'M PART COLOUR BLIND, EVIL MASTER...

EVIL MASTER! I CAN'T SEE YOU!
EUGENE. YOU NEED TO STOP TALKING.

THANKS TO YOUR NON-EXISTENT MINION PEA OF A BRAIN, WE'RE ABOUT TO FACE OUR BIGGEST FEARS!
OH NO. THAT MEANS...

OH HEY THERE.

EUGENE.

NOOOOOO!
JELLY BABIES!!!

OH NO... IT'S HAPPENING!

YOU'VE BEEN A BAD BOY.

GULP
M-M-MOTHER...

YOU'RE JUST AN ILLUSION... YOU'RE NOT REAL...

TIME FOR YOUR BATH, LITTLE PENGUIN OF MINE...
GAAAAAAAH!

NO, NO, NO, NO, NO...

BOSH!

AAAAAH

OH, THANK THE JELLYFISH... IT'S YOU!

THEY'RE EVERYWHERE, EVIL MASTER!
EVERYWHERE!!!

I HAVE TO STOP THE FEARSOMITRON!
BUT THE FEAR FOAM IS SO THICK I HAVE NO IDEA WHERE IT IS!
NO MORE JELLY BABIES! PLEASE, NO MORE...

OH HEY, EUGENE...

OI! EUGENE! GET BACK HERE!

YOU CAN'T LEAVE ME HERE ALONE WHEN MY MOTHER IS LURK-
YOU'RE IN BIG TROUBLE.
OH, GEE...

YOU LEFT YOUR UNDERWEAR ALL OVER THE FLOOR.
I DIDN'T DO IT!!!

MEANWHILE
BUT WE LOVE YOU, EUGENE...

GET AWAY FROM ME, YOU BARBARIANS!
BOMP
DON'T BE SCARED, EUGENE.

FEARSOMITRON EMERGENCY SELF-DESTRUCT BUTTON

FEARSOMITRON EMERGENCY SELF-DESTRUCT BUTTON
PING
WELL, WHAT HAVE WE HERE?

FIND SOMETHING YOU NEED, EUGENE?
BUT IF YOU PRESS IT, WE WON'T GET TO BE FRIENDS...

THEY'RE JUST TINY JELLY SWEETS THAT LOOK LIKE CREEPY BABIES, EUGENE...
THERE'S NOTHING TO BE SCARED OF...

AND WE CAN'T HAVE THAT NOW, CAN WE?!

STEP AWAY FROM THE BUTTON, EDIBLE FIEND!

OR WHAT...?!

NOM
MUNCH
NOM
RIP
CRUNCH

FEARSOMITRON EMERGENCY SELF-DESTRUCT BUTTON
BAM

BOOM

EVERYTHING OKAY IN THERE, SIR?
YES, NUMBER 8...
EVERYTHING IS...
SPIFFING.

CAT-ASTROPHE

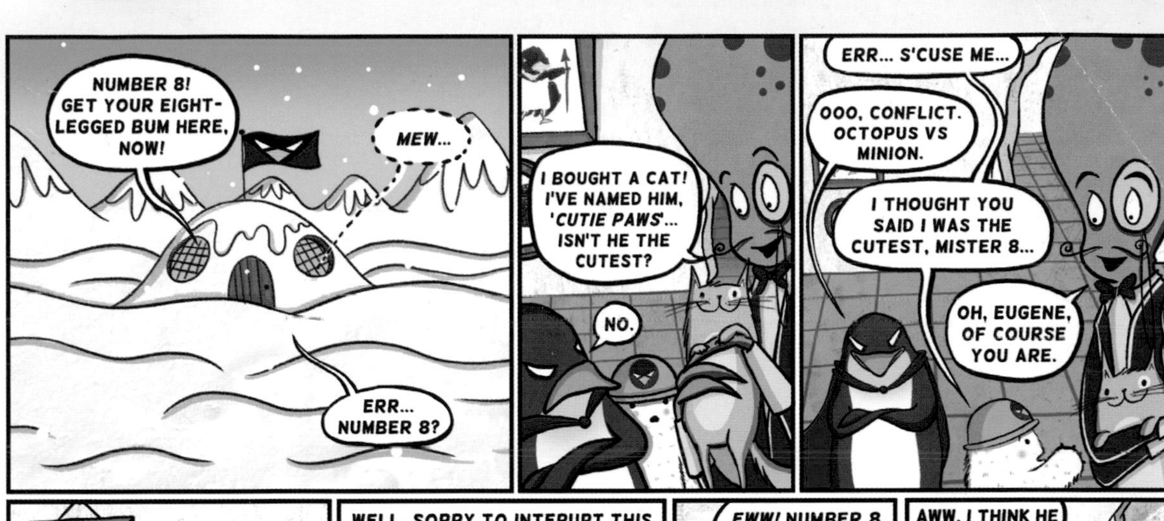

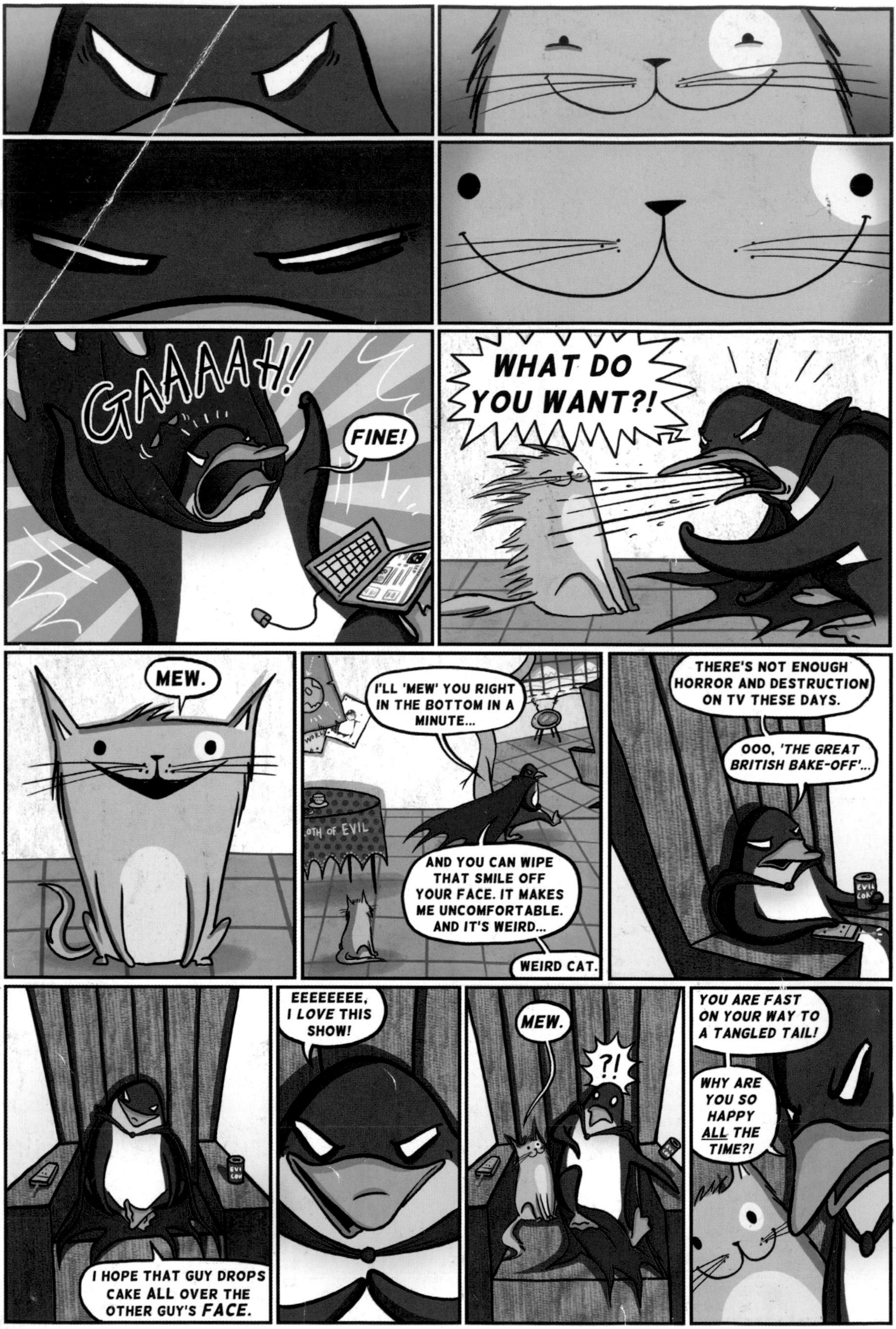

GAAAAH!

FINE!

WHAT DO YOU WANT?!

I KNOW SOMETHING YOU DON'T KNOW...

YOU'RE A ... T-T-TALKING CAT?!

AND YOU'RE A TALKING PENGUIN...
BRAVO! AREN'T WE CLEVER?!

?!

W-W-WHERE DID YOU GO...?
I'M NOT S-S-SCARED OF YOU! C-C-CAT!

WHAT THE JUMPING JIMINIES IS THAT CAT UP TO?!
CORRIDOR OF EVIL
HE MAKES MY FEATHERS CRAWL.

C'MON, EEP, BE BRAVE. HE'S JUST A MEASLY KITTY CAT!
SHOW YOURSELF, YOU STINKING FELINE! I KNOW YOU'RE AROUND HERE SOMEWHERE!

AH-HA!
FOUND YOU!!!
OH!

GOOD GRIEF, EUGENE. WHAT ARE YOU DOING IN THE CORRIDOR OF EVIL?!
I W-W-WAS GOING TO THE TOILET, EVIL MASTER...
WELL... LOOKS LIKE YOU'VE TAKEN CARE OF THAT ALREADY. AS YOU WERE.

AAAAH... YOU'RE MINE NOW.
ONE... TWO... THREE...

HUZZAH!!!
WAIT... WHAAAT?
?!

YOU'RE WASTING YOUR TIME, LITTLE PENGUIN.
YOU WON'T FIND ME, UNTIL I FIND YOU...

Y'SEE, WE'RE NOT SO DIFFERENT Y'KNOW...

YOU!!!
COME CLOSER SO I CAN MAKE A CAT-PANCAKE!
AND WHERE DID YOU GET THAT BRILLIANT, EVIL MOUSTACHE?!
OH, DO CHILL OUT. YOU'RE SO UPTIGHT. NO WONDER YOU NEVER SUCCEED...

NEVER SUCCEED?! HOW DARE YOU!
WELL, HAVE YOU ACTUALLY TAKEN OVER THE WORLD YET?
NO. I DIDN'T THINK SO.

...WHICH MAKES ME A VERY HAPPY CAT. AND THAT IS WHY I'M ALWAYS SMILING.
I SHALL SUCCEED WHERE YOU HAVE SO MISERABLY FAILED!

YOU CAN'T TAKE OVER THE WORLD...

YOU DON'T HAVE A MENACING CAPE...
I DO HAVE A TOP HAT...
GOOD POINT.

EVIL MASTER! WHERE ARE YOU? MISTER 8 WANTS YOU...
HE CAN'T FIND CUTIE PAWS...

HE'S RIGHT H-
...NOT AGAIN.

DO YOU KNOW WHAT'S HAPPENED TO CUTIE PAWS?

I DO BELIEVE "CUTIE PAWS" IS MY NEW ARCH-NEMESIS...
EVIL CAT.

WORLD WIDE WEB

NUMBER 8! GET YOUR SQUID-FACE IN HERE!

NOW!

CAN I COME IN, EVIL MASTER?

YOU MAY AS WELL, EUGENE. I COULD USE YOU AS BAIT...

LET ME PRESENT TO YOU, MY LATEST EVIL INVENTION...

OOO! MORE EVIL STUFF. YAY!

THE SPIDER-BOT 4000!!!

WHY 4000?

ADDING NUMBERS MAKES IT SOUND MORE EVIL. ESPECIALLY THOUSANDS.

THE SPIDER-BOT 4000 HAS THE ABILITY TO BUILD INDESTRUCTIBLE SPIDER WEBS, PERFECT FOR CATCHING HUMANS JUST LIKE TINY PATHETIC FLIES!

ONCE UNLEASHED, THE SPIDER-BOTS CAN GET TO WORK AND I'LL BE WELL ON MY WAY TO *TAKING OVER THE WORLD!!!*

SCUTTLE
SCUTTLE
SCUTTLE
SCUTTLE
SCUTTLE
SCUTTLE
SCUTTLE
SCUTTLE
WELL. THAT JUST RUINED MY DAY.
NEW YORK
QUICK, I'D BETTER TWEET THIS!
LIKE...WHOA!
OKAY, EVERYONE, JUST STAY CALM AND TRY NOT TO MOVE...
WE CAN'T MOVE ANYWAY!
LONDON
I AM NOT AMUSED!
GOLLY.
PARIS
MY BAGUETTES ARE RUINED!
OH, PIERRE, MAYBE IT'S A WEB OF LOVE! HOW ROMANTIC...
NO, DEAR... IT'S REALLY NOT.
ITALY
HMMM, ADRIANO! ZIS PASTA IZZA DELIIIICIOUS!
ZAT'S... NOT... PASTA...
IT'S WORKING, NUMBER 8!!!
THE SPIDER-BOTS HAVE CREATED QUITE THE WEB-IDEMIC!!!

WORLD DOMINATION IS A PIECE OF CAKE.
I MIGHT CHANGE MY NAME TO LORD HUMPLEDINK.
CONTROL PANEL OF EVIL
JUST ROLLS OFF THE TONGUE.

CONTROL
OH, FOR CRYING OUT LOUD. NOT YOU AGAIN...
THE SPIDER-BOTS WILL GET YOU SOON ENOUGH, EVIL CAT!
IS THAT WHAT THEY'RE CALLING ME THESE DAYS?

PEW
PEW
PEW
PEW
PEW

HE DIDN'T...

NUMBER 8! GRAB THE KEYS TO THE FLYING POD OF EVIL!
MY WEB-PLAN IS BEING FOILED BY THAT SMALL FURRY FREAK OF A CAT. WE NEED TO GO STOP HIM, NOW!

NEW YORK
DON'T YOU THINK YOU SHOULD SLOW DOWN, SIR?
YOU NEED TO MAKE SURE WE DON'T GET-
FLYING POD OF EVIL

...CAUGHT.

WELL... WHAT NOW?
YOU'RE MEANT TO BE THE WISE SQUID...

GOT YOURSELF CAUGHT UP IN YOUR OWN WEB OF DESTRUCTION I SEE.
WHY DON'T WE GET THIS OVER WITH, EH?

I'M AFRAID I HAD TO DESTROY YOUR SPIDER-BOTS AS THEY WERE MAKING SUCH A MESS.

AND NOW I'M GOING TO HAVE TO DESTROY YOU.

GULP

MEANWHILE AT EEP HQ...
YOU READY, EUGENE?!
OKAY, JOHN!
ONE... TWO... THREE!

BAM!

BIG RED EVIL BUTTON
BEEP!
OH NO... NOT THE BIG RED EVIL BUTTON!!!

DID WE DIE YET?
NOTHING HAPPENED. HOW BORING.

NEW YORK
WHAT ON EARTH...

NAY
NAY
NAY
NAY
NAY
NAY
IT'S LIKE BEING IN THE CUTEST NIGHTMARE EVER...
NAY
NAY

OKAY... WHO PRESSED THE BIG RED EVIL BUTTON...?
YOUR BIG RED EVIL BUTTON RELEASES... UNICORNS?

I'M STILL WORKING ON ITS EVIL-NESS...
I HAVE TO SAY, IT'S QUITE A BEAUTIFUL SIGHT.

AND THAT WAS THAT!
WINK

The Truce: Part 1

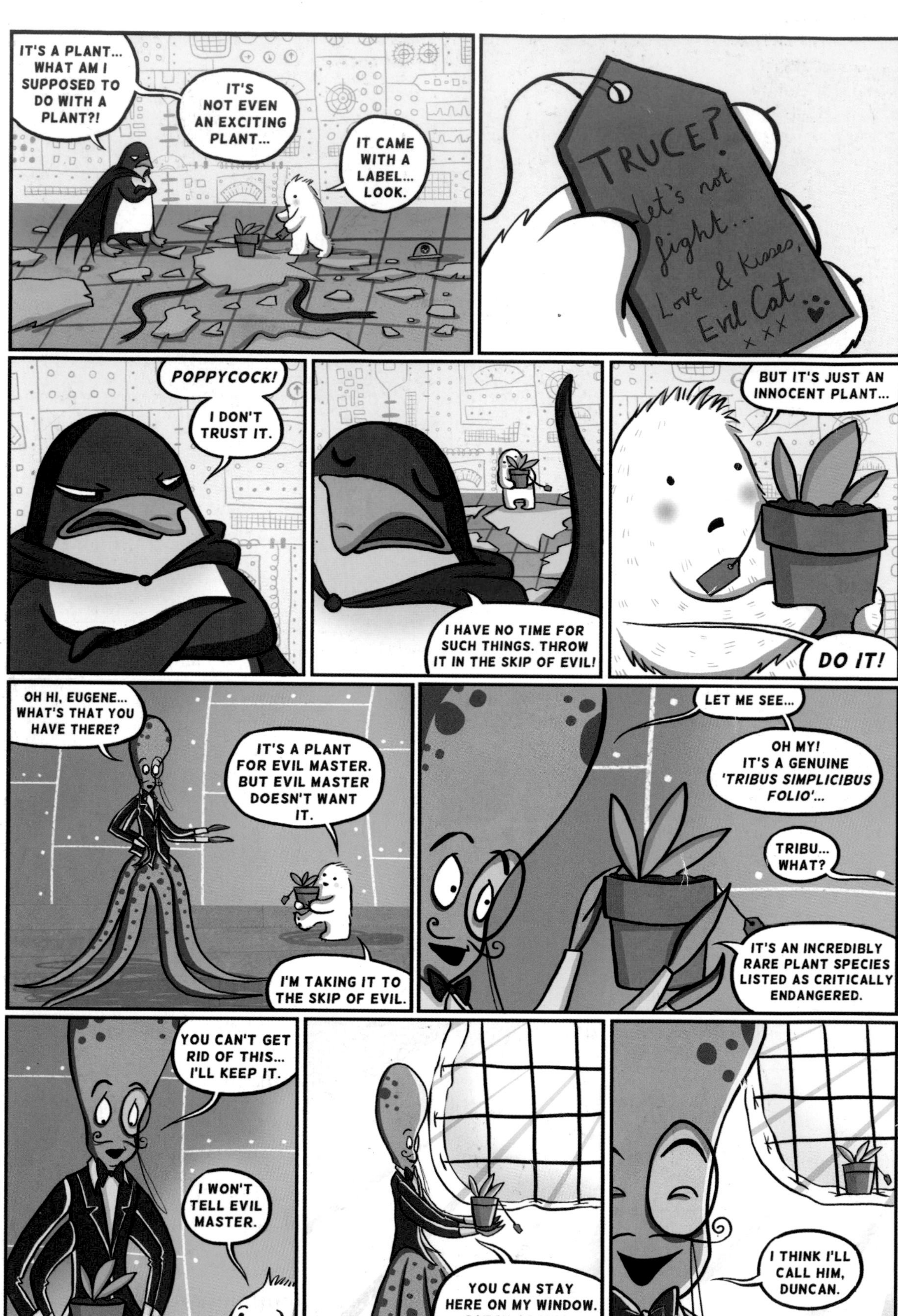
IT'S A PLANT... WHAT AM I SUPPOSED TO DO WITH A PLANT?!
IT'S NOT EVEN AN EXCITING PLANT...
IT CAME WITH A LABEL... LOOK.
TRUCE? let's not fight... Love & Kisses, Evil Cat xxx
POPPYCOCK!
I DON'T TRUST IT.
I HAVE NO TIME FOR SUCH THINGS. THROW IT IN THE SKIP OF EVIL!
BUT IT'S JUST AN INNOCENT PLANT...
DO IT!
OH HI, EUGENE... WHAT'S THAT YOU HAVE THERE?
IT'S A PLANT FOR EVIL MASTER. BUT EVIL MASTER DOESN'T WANT IT.
I'M TAKING IT TO THE SKIP OF EVIL.
LET ME SEE...
OH MY! IT'S A GENUINE *'TRIBUS SIMPLICIBUS FOLIO'*...
TRIBU... WHAT?
IT'S AN INCREDIBLY RARE PLANT SPECIES LISTED AS CRITICALLY ENDANGERED.
YOU CAN'T GET RID OF THIS... I'LL KEEP IT.
I WON'T TELL EVIL MASTER.
YOU CAN STAY HERE ON MY WINDOW. CATCH AS MUCH LIGHT AS YOU CAN...
I THINK I'LL CALL HIM, DUNCAN.

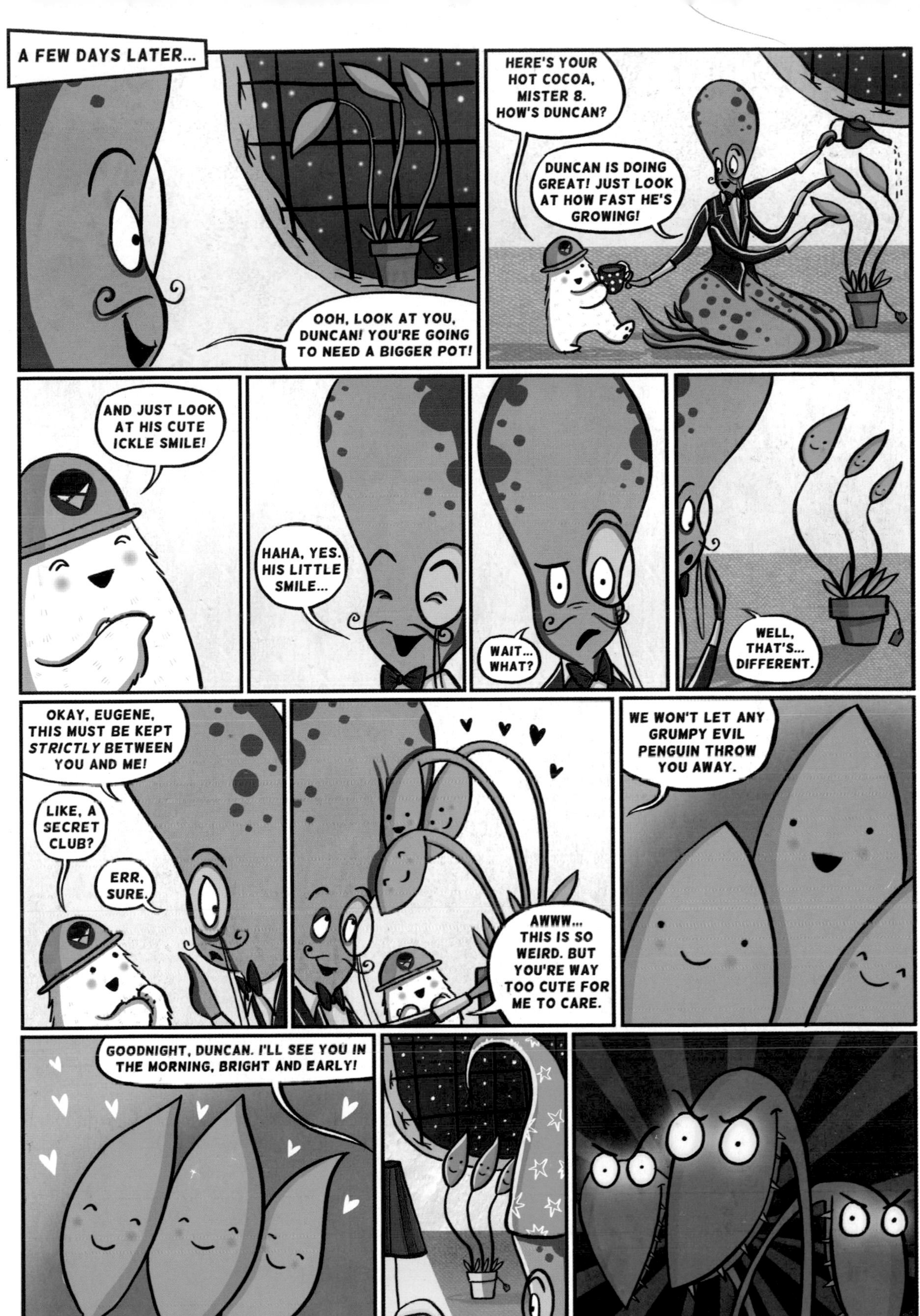
A FEW DAYS LATER...
OOH, LOOK AT YOU, DUNCAN! YOU'RE GOING TO NEED A BIGGER POT!
HERE'S YOUR HOT COCOA, MISTER 8. HOW'S DUNCAN?
DUNCAN IS DOING GREAT! JUST LOOK AT HOW FAST HE'S GROWING!
AND JUST LOOK AT HIS CUTE ICKLE SMILE!
HAHA, YES. HIS LITTLE SMILE...
WAIT... WHAT?
WELL, THAT'S... DIFFERENT.
OKAY, EUGENE, THIS MUST BE KEPT STRICTLY BETWEEN YOU AND ME!
LIKE, A SECRET CLUB?
ERR, SURE.
AWWW... THIS IS SO WEIRD. BUT YOU'RE WAY TOO CUTE FOR ME TO CARE.
WE WON'T LET ANY GRUMPY EVIL PENGUIN THROW YOU AWAY.
GOODNIGHT, DUNCAN. I'LL SEE YOU IN THE MORNING, BRIGHT AND EARLY!

PING
WHO'S THERE?
PING
NUMBER 8, IS THAT YOU?
THUD
THUD
THUD
CREEEEAAAK...
EEG'S ROOM
KEEP OUT
BLAAARG!

THE TRUCE: PART 2

PREVIOUSLY ON EEP...

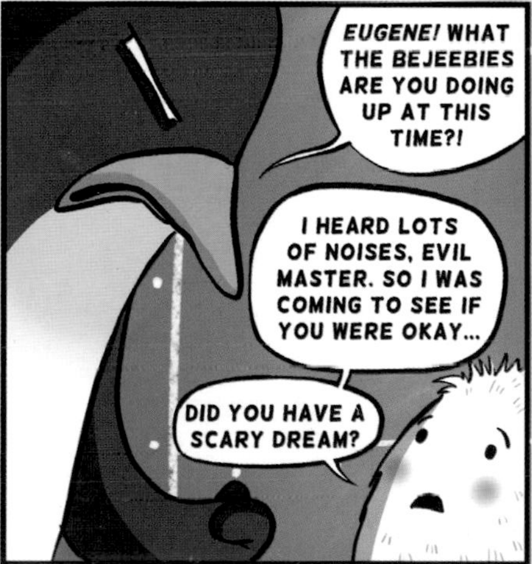

OH, HELLO, FRIEND!

THIS IS THE PART WHERE YOU **RUN!**
I DON'T THINK IT WANTS TO BE FRIENDS.

QUICK! IT SHOULDN'T FIND US IN HERE. PLUS, WITHOUT HANDS, THERE'S NO WAY IT CAN GET IN.
KITCHEN OF EVIL
IT LOOKED FAMILIAR...

ARE WE GOING TO GET EATEN, EVIL MASTER?
PROBABLY.

IT'S FOUND US!
WELL, IT SHOULDN'T BE ABLE TO TURN THE HANDLE...
JIGGLE
JIGGLE
JIGGLE
OKAY... IT'S TURNING THE HANDLE.

DON'T LET IT **SEE** YOU!
IT LOOKS HUNGRY.

KEEP STILL AND VERY QUIET.
MY NOSE IS TICKLING...
JUST DON'T-

AACHOO!

I THINK I NEED A HANKY.

IT'S OKAY, EVIL MASTER. I THINK THE SCARY PLANT MONSTER HAS GONE...

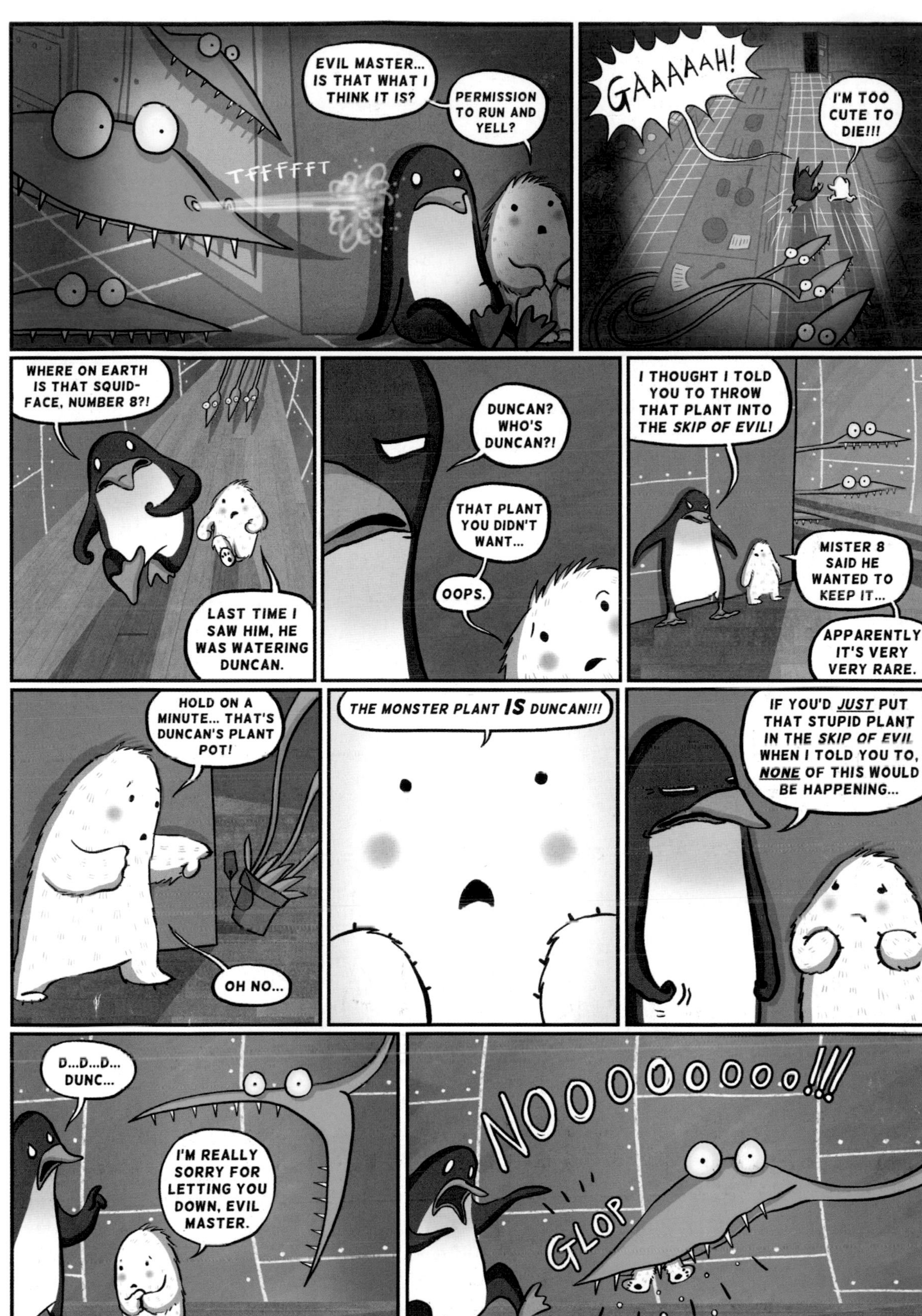
EVIL MASTER... IS THAT WHAT I THINK IT IS?
PERMISSION TO RUN AND YELL?
TFFFFFT
GAAAAAH!
I'M TOO CUTE TO DIE!!!
WHERE ON EARTH IS THAT SQUID-FACE, NUMBER 8?!
LAST TIME I SAW HIM, HE WAS WATERING DUNCAN.
DUNCAN? WHO'S DUNCAN?!
THAT PLANT YOU DIDN'T WANT...
OOPS.
I THOUGHT I TOLD YOU TO THROW THAT PLANT INTO THE *SKIP OF EVIL*!
MISTER 8 SAID HE WANTED TO KEEP IT...
APPARENTLY IT'S VERY VERY RARE.
HOLD ON A MINUTE... THAT'S DUNCAN'S PLANT POT!
OH NO...
THE MONSTER PLANT ***IS*** *DUNCAN!!!*
IF YOU'D *JUST* PUT THAT STUPID PLANT IN THE *SKIP OF EVIL* WHEN I TOLD YOU TO, *NONE* OF THIS WOULD BE HAPPENING...
D...D...D... DUNC...
I'M REALLY SORRY FOR LETTING YOU DOWN, EVIL MASTER.
NOOOOOOOO!!!
GLOP

Y...Y...YOU ATE EUGENE...
YOU JUST WENT ALONG AND GOBBLED HIM RIGHT UP...

NO!
WHAT THE...

I WILL NOT PUT UP WITH THIS!

I SHALL NOT BE EATEN!!!

SHWOOOOOOP

DOOF
BOOF
EUGENE HAS TOO MUCH TO LIVE FOR!
BAM

WHAAAAAT...?
NOW, YOU THINK ABOUT YOUR ACTIONS, YOU BAD BAD PLANT!

HEY GUYS, WHAT'S GOIN- OH... DUNCAN?!
YOU!
EXPLAIN YOURSELF, SQUIDMITTS!
WHAT?!
DUNCAN HAS BEEN VERY NAUGHTY, MISTER 8.

HOW WAS I MEANT TO KNOW IT WAS AN EVIL PLANT?!
YOU KNOW NOTHING, NUMBER 8.
WELL, AT LEAST WE'RE ALL FINE. SO IT'S A HAPPY ENDING, RIGHT?!
ERR, SURE.

SFFMMM

I HAVE GOT TO ELIMINATE THAT RIDICULOUSLY CUTE MINION.
ON
EYE OF THE PLANT
EVIL PLAN: FAIL
THIS ISN'T THE END, EVIL PENGUIN. I WILL PREVAIL NEXT TIME!!!

THE STINKING TRUTH

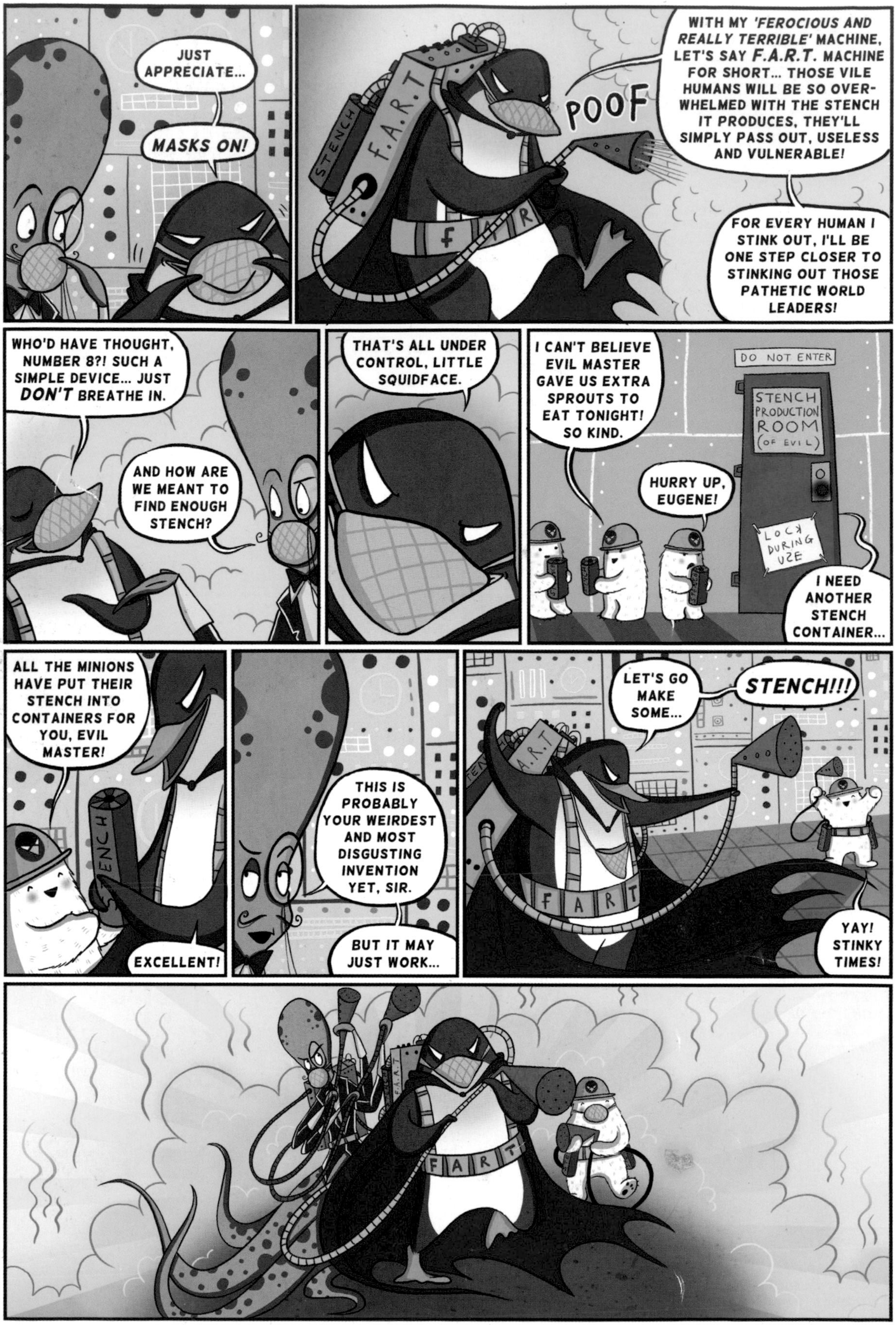

JUST APPRECIATE...

MASKS ON!

POOF

WITH MY *'FEROCIOUS AND REALLY TERRIBLE'* MACHINE, LET'S SAY ***F.A.R.T.*** MACHINE FOR SHORT... THOSE VILE HUMANS WILL BE SO OVERWHELMED WITH THE STENCH IT PRODUCES, THEY'LL SIMPLY PASS OUT, USELESS AND VULNERABLE!

FOR EVERY HUMAN I STINK OUT, I'LL BE ONE STEP CLOSER TO STINKING OUT THOSE PATHETIC WORLD LEADERS!

WHO'D HAVE THOUGHT, NUMBER 8?! SUCH A SIMPLE DEVICE... JUST ***DON'T*** BREATHE IN.

AND HOW ARE WE MEANT TO FIND ENOUGH STENCH?

THAT'S ALL UNDER CONTROL, LITTLE SQUIDFACE.

DO NOT ENTER

STENCH PRODUCTION ROOM (OF EVIL)

I CAN'T BELIEVE EVIL MASTER GAVE US EXTRA SPROUTS TO EAT TONIGHT! SO KIND.

HURRY UP, EUGENE!

LOCK DURING USE

I NEED ANOTHER STENCH CONTAINER...

ALL THE MINIONS HAVE PUT THEIR STENCH INTO CONTAINERS FOR YOU, EVIL MASTER!

EXCELLENT!

THIS IS PROBABLY YOUR WEIRDEST AND MOST DISGUSTING INVENTION YET, SIR.

BUT IT MAY JUST WORK...

LET'S GO MAKE SOME...

STENCH!!!

YAY! STINKY TIMES!

TICKETS
THREE TICKETS TO 'STINKSVILLE', PLEASE!
TRAINS
VERY FUNNY. STOP WASTING MY TIME.
ENOUGH OF THAT *STINKING* ATTITUDE!
POOF
POOF
DOES THIS TRAIN CARRIAGE SMELL A BIT FUNNY TO YOU?
IT DOES NOW!!!
POOF
POOF
POOF
POOF
POOF
POOF
TRAINS TO THE CITY
POOF
POOF
POOF
POOF
POOF
POOF
POOF
POOF
POOF
POOF
THIS IS TOO EASY!
WAIT A MINUTE...
IT'S STOPPED *POOFING!*
C'MON!!! WORK!
EUGENE, CAN YOU SEE WHAT'S GOING ON WITH MY F.A.R.T. MACHINE?!
THE BLASTED THING HAS STOPPED POOFING OUT ANY STENCH...
OH NO! YOU'VE GOT A STENCH BUILD UP, EVIL MASTER!
RUMBLE
WHAT?!
RUMBLE
STENCH
F.A.R.T.
RUMBLE
GET THIS THING OFF OF ME, EUGENE!
QUICK!!!
I'M TRYING!
IT'S GONNA BLOW!!!
WE'D BETTER——
STENCH
POOF
RUUUUN!!!
IT'S A NUCLEAR STENCH CLOUD!!!

OOOF!!!

OUCHIES! MY ANKLE... I CAN'T MOVE IT...

EVIL MASTER!!! HELP ME!
I CAN'T WALK! I'VE HURT MY ANKLE!

HELP ME! THE NUCLEAR STENCH CLOUD IS GETTING CLOSER!

EVIL MASTER...?
HE... HE LEFT ME...

OH NO!

DEEP BREATHS, EUGENE. IT ALL HAD TO END SOME TIME...

YOINK
SWOOOP

EVIL CAT?!
HOLD TIGHT, TINY EUGENE. I'M OPENING THE TRAP DOOR...

YOU SAVED ME...
DID THAT MEAN OL' PENGUIN LEAVE YOU TO GET STENCHED?!
I'D NEVER TREAT MY TOP MINION IN SUCH A TERRIBLE MANNER!

IF YOU WERE MY MINION, I'D NEVER EVER LEAVE YOU. HOW ABOUT IT, EUGENE? YOU COULD WORK FOR ME NOW...
YOU'D GET A SHINY NEW HAT... IN BLUE.

Helpmeeee!

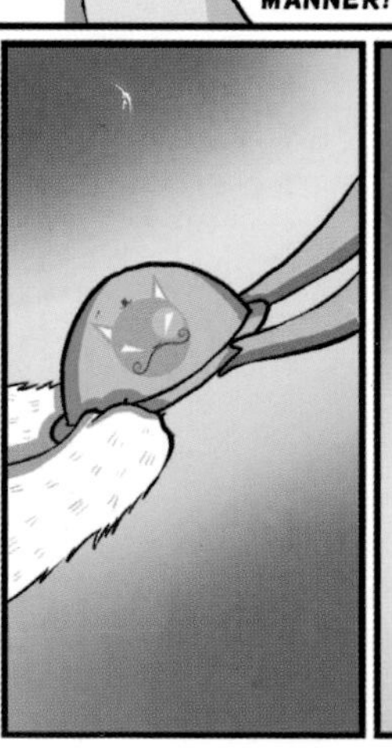

YOU WON'T REGRET THIS DECISION, EUGENE.

PLEASE ALIGHT FOR THE DOMINATION STATION: PART 1

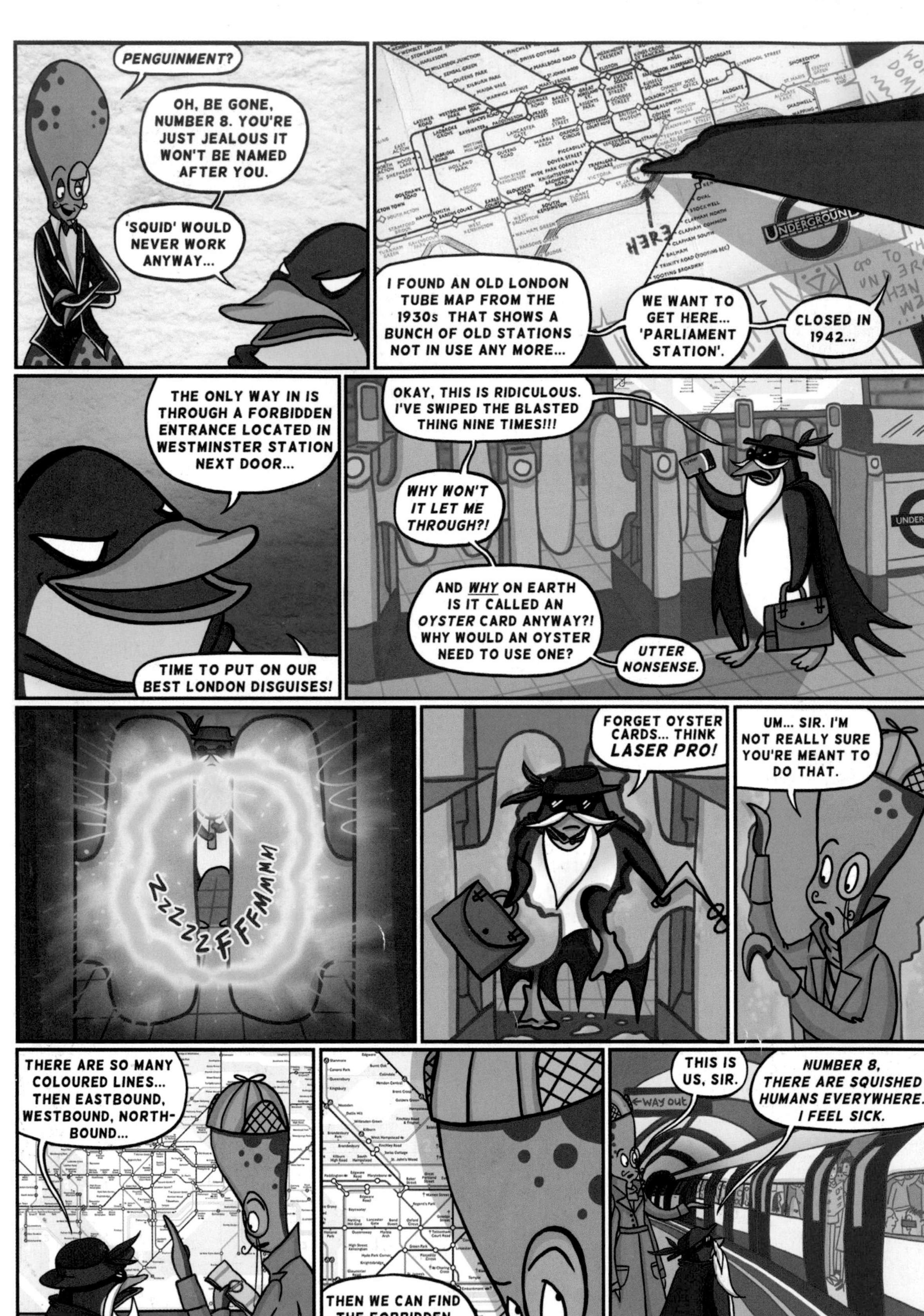
PENGUINMENT?
OH, BE GONE, NUMBER 8. YOU'RE JUST JEALOUS IT WON'T BE NAMED AFTER YOU.
'SQUID' WOULD NEVER WORK ANYWAY...
I FOUND AN OLD LONDON TUBE MAP FROM THE 1930s THAT SHOWS A BUNCH OF OLD STATIONS NOT IN USE ANY MORE...
WE WANT TO GET HERE... 'PARLIAMENT STATION'.
CLOSED IN 1942...
HERE
UNDERGROUND
THE ONLY WAY IN IS THROUGH A FORBIDDEN ENTRANCE LOCATED IN WESTMINSTER STATION NEXT DOOR...
TIME TO PUT ON OUR BEST LONDON DISGUISES!
OKAY, THIS IS RIDICULOUS. I'VE SWIPED THE BLASTED THING NINE TIMES!!!
WHY WON'T IT LET ME THROUGH?!
AND WHY ON EARTH IS IT CALLED AN OYSTER CARD ANYWAY?! WHY WOULD AN OYSTER NEED TO USE ONE?
UTTER NONSENSE.
ZZZZZFFFMMMM
FORGET OYSTER CARDS... THINK LASER PRO!
UM... SIR. I'M NOT REALLY SURE YOU'RE MEANT TO DO THAT.
THERE ARE SO MANY COLOURED LINES... THEN EASTBOUND, WESTBOUND, NORTH-BOUND...
WE NEED TO GO WESTBOUND ON THE GREEN LINE.
THEN WE CAN FIND THE FORBIDDEN DOORWAY TO THE ABANDONED PARLIAMENT STATION. EASY!
WAY OUT
THIS IS US, SIR.
NUMBER 8, THERE ARE SQUISHED HUMANS EVERYWHERE. I FEEL SICK.

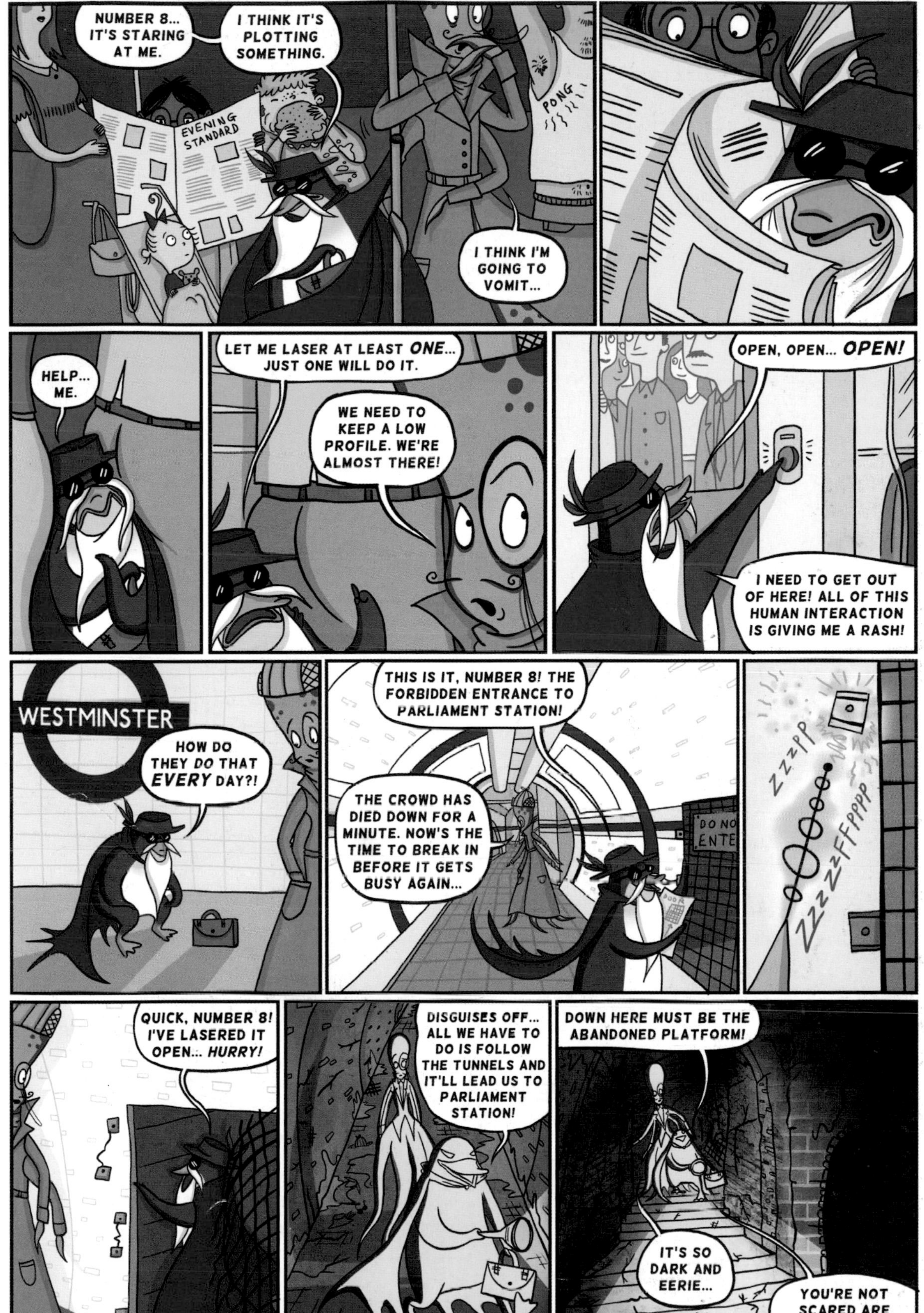
NUMBER 8... IT'S STARING AT ME.
I THINK IT'S PLOTTING SOMETHING.
EVENING STANDARD
PONG
I THINK I'M GOING TO VOMIT...
HELP... ME.
LET ME LASER AT LEAST ONE... JUST ONE WILL DO IT.
WE NEED TO KEEP A LOW PROFILE. WE'RE ALMOST THERE!
OPEN, OPEN... OPEN!
I NEED TO GET OUT OF HERE! ALL OF THIS HUMAN INTERACTION IS GIVING ME A RASH!
WESTMINSTER
HOW DO THEY DO THAT EVERY DAY?!
THIS IS IT, NUMBER 8! THE FORBIDDEN ENTRANCE TO PARLIAMENT STATION!
THE CROWD HAS DIED DOWN FOR A MINUTE. NOW'S THE TIME TO BREAK IN BEFORE IT GETS BUSY AGAIN...
ZZZPP
ZZZZFFPPPP
QUICK, NUMBER 8! I'VE LASERED IT OPEN... HURRY!
DISGUISES OFF... ALL WE HAVE TO DO IS FOLLOW THE TUNNELS AND IT'LL LEAD US TO PARLIAMENT STATION!
DOWN HERE MUST BE THE ABANDONED PLATFORM!
IT'S SO DARK AND EERIE...
YOU'RE NOT SCARED ARE YOU, NUMBER 8?!

OH, HE SHOULD BE...

HELLO BOYS.
EVIL CAT!!!

AND EUGENE! MY TOP MINION! YOU'RE ALIVE!

I'M NOT YOUR MINION ANY MORE!
EVIL CAT IS MY EVIL MASTER.

NO!
BUT, EUGENE... EVIL CAT IS OUR ARCH-NEMESIS!

THAT'S RIGHT, BOYS! HE FINALLY CAME TO HIS SENSES AND PICKED THE RIGHT SIDE OF EVIL.

THE SIDE OF VICTORY!

EUGENE... WHY?

AT THE NUCLEAR FART A MONTH AGO, I WAS IN TROUBLE...
BUT EVIL EMPEROR PENGUIN LEFT ME BEHIND... TO BECOME STENCHED.
THE NUCLEAR FART WAS A MILLIMETRE AWAY...THEN EVIL CAT SAVED ME.

IS THIS TRUE, SIR?? YOU LEFT HIM TO GET STENCHED?!
MAYBE A LITTLE BIT...

LOOK, GUYS, I'M EVIL EMPEROR PENGUIN. I'M EVIL. DON'T TAKE IT PERSONALLY!
YOU'RE BEING WAY TOO SENSITIVE, EUGENE. YOU'RE ALIVE NOW, THAT'S THE MAIN THING...
AM I RIGHT?!

I'M BORED NOW. EUGENE... TIME TO USE THE CUPCAKE.

CUPCAKE...?

WHOOOOSH
HUP

SIR... THAT'S NO CUPCAKE...
TICK TICK TICK

Please Alight for the Domination Station: Part 2

Previously, in an abandoned underground station...

This guy...

Ran into this guy...

And this guy...

Threw this...

And it started doing this...

TICK
TICK
TICK

ARGH! AND NOW THE JELLYFISH AND HIS PENGUIN HAVE GOTTEN AWAY!
HURRY!
PARLIAMENT STATION

OKAY... MY NEW 'WHISKERS 2000' TRACKING DEVICE SHOULD DETECT ANY SIGNS OF MOVEMENT IN THE TUNNELS.
OOO, CLEVER.

I SEE THEM!
OOO, AND THEY'RE MOVING SUPER FAST... AND COMING STRAIGHT FOR US... HOW CONVENIENT.

HOLD ON A MINUTE... THAT'S A-

TRAAAIN!

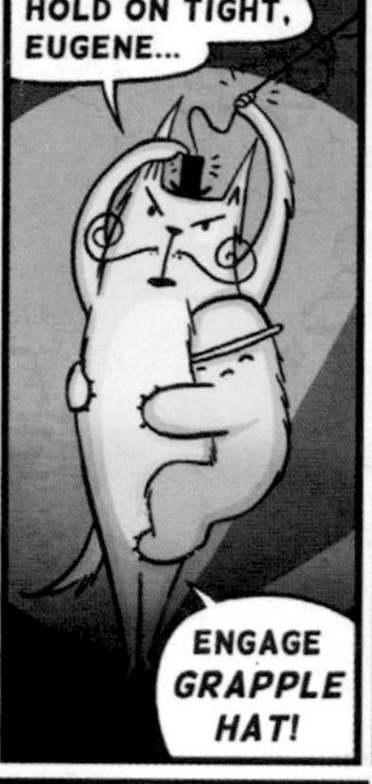
HOLD ON TIGHT, EUGENE...
ENGAGE GRAPPLE HAT!

WHOOOOOOSH

MEANWHILE...
WE CAN'T JUST LEAVE EUGENE BEHIND WITH EVIL CAT!
SURE WE CAN.

ANYWAY, EUGENE WILL PROBABLY FINISH OFF EVIL CAT HIMSELF.
DEATH BY CUTE OVERLOAD.
HA!

I THOUGHT THAT WAS QUITE WITTY. WHY AREN'T YOU LAUGHING, NUMBER 8?!
NUMBER 8...?

OH, HE'S LAUGHING, DON'T YOU WORRY...
H-HAR?
WITH FEAR!

ERGH, YOU AGAIN. YOU'RE LIKE A BAD SMELL THAT WON'T LEAVE.
YOU DON'T SOUND PLEASED TO SEE ME. I FIND THAT QUITE RUDE. DON'T YOU THINK THAT'S QUITE RUDE, NUMBER 8?

DOOBEE DOO...

YOU HESITATED!!!

YOU NEED TO TEACH YOUR JELLYFISH SOME MANNERS!
IT'S SQUID... AND WHY WOULD ANYONE BE PLEASED TO SEE YOU?!

RUDE!
YOU HURT MY FEELINGS...

HOW DID YOU COPE WITH THAT PENGUIN FOR SO LONG, EUGENE...?!
I DON'T BLAME YOU FOR LEAVING.
MAYBE I SHOULD SEE HOW MUCH THE JELLYFISH REALLY MEANS TO HIM...

CLICK
1, 2, 3...

ZAP!

NOOOOO!

WHAT THE?!
?
OH, YAY! IT WORKS!
CLOUDS!

EUGENE!
WHY DO I HAVE A FEELING YOU ARE RESPONSIBLE FOR THIS?!

BECAUSE I AM, SILLY BILLY!
I CALL IT 'LASER OF DREEEAMS'.

FINE!
LAUNCH SUPER FLAME GRENADES!
COOKED JELLYFISH IS ON THE MENU!

FLUTTER
FLUTTER
FLUTTER
FLUTTER
PING
PING
PING

MY TRUSTY POISON PISTOL SHOULD DO THE TRICK!
PREPARE TO BE JELLYFISH JUICE!!!

SPLURGE

YAY!
JAM!

BAZOOKA IN YOUR FACE!

WHAA-
BOOM
MOO?

I CALL IT A BA'MOO'KAH!

BAAAAAH!

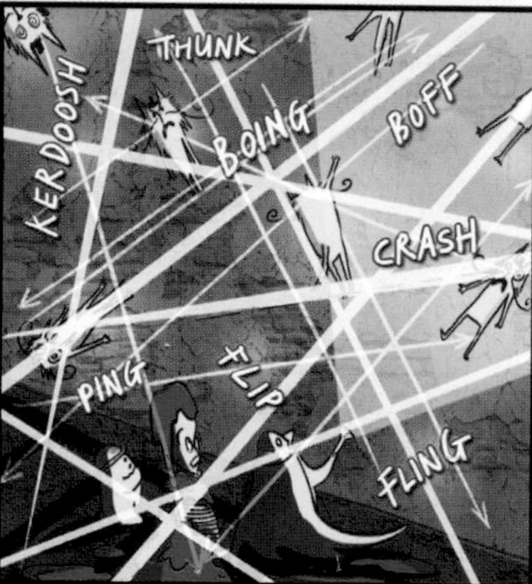
KERDOOSH
THUNK
BOING
BOFF
CRASH
PING
FLIP
FLING

MEOW.

EVIL MASTER?
HE ACTUALLY DID IT... CUTE OVER-LOAD FINISHED OFF EVIL CAT.
PUUURR
PUURR
PURR
PURR
WOULD ANYONE CARE FOR SOME PLUM JAM?

WE CAN BE FRIENDS FOREVER!

HEAD IN THE CLOUDS

EVIL CAT'S EVIL BASE
EVIL MASTER. DO I HAVE TO WEAR THIS MOUSTACHE?
IT'S TICKLING MY NOSE...
YOU KNOW THE RULES, EUGENE...
THE TOP HAT AND MOUSTACHE ARE COMPULSORY WHEN YOU'RE WORKING INSIDE MY EVIL BASE... ARE YOU TELLING ME THAT YOU DON'T THINK THEY LOOK FABULOUS?
BECAUSE THAT WOULD MEAN YOU DON'T THINK I LOOK FABULOUS... IS THAT WHAT YOU'RE SAYING, EUGENE?!
ERM, NO, EVIL MASTER. I MEAN, YES... YOU LOOK FABULOUS. IT'S ALL... FABULOUS.
GOOD. NOW, WE MUST FOCUS, EUGENE. AFTER ALL, I HAVE INVENTED THE ULTIMATE DEVICE TO SPY ON THAT PUNY PENGUIN AND HIS PLANS.
AND YOU ARE MY MOST IMPORTANT PART.
OOO, I LIKE BEING IMPORTANT PARTS!
IT ONLY REQUIRES EVAPORATING YOU A TEENSY BIT.
WELL, THAT'S OKIE DOKIE THEN!
BEHOLD! THE NEW AND BRILLIANT 'EVAPOR-TRANSPORTER-POD'... EVIL CAT EDITION.
YOU STEP INSIDE THE MACHINE, AND STAND VERY STILL... I MUST REITERATE, VERY STILL. NO MOVING. AT ALL.
YOU WILL THEN BE EVAPORATED AND TRANSPORTED TO THE DESIRED LOCATION... IN THIS CASE, EVIL EMPEROR PENGUIN'S HEADQUARTERS...
...WHERE YOU CAN THEN SPY ON ALL OF THAT PENGUIN'S EVIL PLANS AND REPORT THEM BACK TO ME.
WELL, EUGENE. YOUR EVAPORATION AWAITS!
RIGHT NOW? BUT WHAT IF EVIL EMPEROR PENGUIN IS EATING DINNER AT THE MOMENT...?

WHY DO YOU CARE?! I COULDN'T CARE LESS IF HE'S SITTING ON THE TOILET...
YOU ARE MY MINION, AND YOU OBEY MY RULES. NOW, LET'S GET TO WORK!
AND REMEMBER... KEEP STILL.
READY, EUGENE?
I THINK SO...
INITIATING HYPER-EVAPORATION...
CO-ORDINATES FOR EVIL EMPEROR PENGUIN'S HQ SET...
AND ACTIVATE!
ZZFFMM
BANG
CLICK
ZZFFM
ZZZP
ZZZP
POP
ZZZP
ZFFMM
HUZZAH! IT IS DONE!
IT IS?! YAY!
...WHAT?!
DID IT WORK?!
AM I EVAPORATED YET?
ERR... NO! BECAUSE YOU'RE STILL HERE!!!
AND YOU'RE A CLOUD!
THERE'S NO NEED TO CALL ME NAMES, EVIL MASTER.
DID YOU STAY STILL LIKE YOU WERE MEANT TO?!
I TRIED TO, EVIL MASTER, BUT I HAD AN ITCHY BOTTOM. SO I THOUGHT I'D QUICKLY SCRATCH IT BEFORE I GOT EVAPORATED...
BUT THEN IT GOT BRIGHT AND I FELT EVER SO LIGHT AND AIRY... SO IT MUST HAVE WORKED, I THOUGHT, BECAUSE I'M LIGHT AND AIRY.

WHY ARE YOU BEING A GRUMPALUMP, EVIL MASTER?
I FEEL GREAT!
GEE, EUGENE... I CAN'T THINK WHY I WOULD BE ANGRY RIGHT NOW.
OOO, LOOK! WHAT A GLORIOUS DAY OUT THERE!
WEEEEEEEE!
NO! EUGENE! DON'T GO OUT THE WINDOW! YOU'LL-
...FLOAT AWAY.
OH, ISN'T THIS JUST LOVELY!
HEY THERE, LITTLE BIRDY.
SWOOOOOSH
HEE HEE!
HOURS LATER...
LA LA LAAR!

SIR. IT'S TIME FOR YOUR YOGA CLASS OF EVIL.
PERISCOPE OF EVIL
NOT JUST YET, NUMBER 8. I'M CHECKING FOR INTRUDERS.
I'M DESPERATE TO TRY OUT MY NEW 'DISINTEGRATOR'.
WHAT THE...?!
I MUST BE OVER-TIRED...
RUB RUB
BUT COULD IT BE...?
...OH.
SIR, ARE YOU OKAY OUT THERE?
AHEM. OF COURSE, NUMBER 8! WHY WOULDN'T I BE?!
SIGH.

SIBLING RIVALRY: PART 1

WHAT EXACTLY DOES MUM THINK I'M DOING AS A CAREER...?
WELL, THAT'S A STUPID QUESTION...
DEPUTY ASSOCIATE ADMINISTRATOR FOR EXPLORATION SYSTEMS AND DEVELOPMENT AT NASA OF COURSE.

WELL... W'DYA KNOW...
SHE BELIEVED ME.

MUM DOESN'T APPROVE OF MY CAREER CHOICE...
WHY?
BECAUSE I'M...

...GOING TO TAKE OVER THE WORLD!!!
AND EVERYONE WILL KNOW ME AS THE EVIL EMPEROR PENGUIN!

NOT ANOTHER ONE...
ERR... NO AND NO.

BUT WHY?! IT'S NOT LIKE YOU'RE PLANNING ON DOING ANYTHING AS AMBITIOUS AS TAKING OVER THE WORLD!!!
WHILST YOU'VE BEEN PLAYING WITH ROCKETS, DOING YOUR BORING ADMINISTRATION STUFF, I'VE BEEN MAKING PLANS!

AND YOU CAN'T STOP ME, BROTHER!

POOF!
HOW DID SHE DO THAT?!

NO DISRESPECT, SIR, BUT YOUR SISTER IS CREEPY.
WE HAVE TO FIND HER BEFORE SHE FINDS THE INVENTION ROOM OF EVIL...

BOOM
OOO, COOL!!! AN INVENTION ROOM OF EVIL!

SIGH...

C'MON, NUMBER 8, LET'S GO!

CORRIDOR OF EVIL
THIS WAY. THAT 'BOOM' SOUNDED SUSPICIOUSLY LIKE THE IGNITION OF THE SONIC RAY GUN I BUILT LAST WEEK...

INVENTION ROOM OF EVIL
CAN YOU SEE ANYTHING, NUMBER 8?

OH HEEEEY!
BONK

UNLOCK THIS DOOR, RIGHT NOW!

I DON'T THINK YOU'VE BEEN TELLING MUM THE WHOLE TRUTH, BROTHER...

THIS DOESN'T LOOK LIKE NASA STUFF TO ME...

YOU'RE INVENTING EVIL STUFF! AND I'M GONNA TELL MUM!!!
DON'T YOU D-
UNLESS...

YOU LET ME JOIN YOU... THEN YOUR SECRET MIGHT BE SAFE.
BUT IF YOU'RE HORRID TO ME, I'M TELLING.

THERE IS NO WAY ON THIS TINY PATHETIC PLANET THAT YOU'RE HAVING ANYTHING TO DO WITH MY WORLD DOMINATION PLANS!

SO, WHAT DOES THIS ACTUALLY DO?! LET'S SEE HOW GOOD YOU REALLY ARE AT THIS EVIL MALARKY!
ZZZZFFM
ZZP ZZP ZZP
IT'S PROBABLY A WISE IDEA IF YOU LEAVE TAKING OVER THE WORLD TO ME.

NO!!! RUTH!

KAH-BOOM

SHE'S JUST BLOWN UP *ALL* MY INVENTIONS...

THAT WAS **AWESOME!!!**

OPEN UP. **OPEN UP.** ***OPEN UP!!!***
INVENTION ROOM OF EVIL

I HOPE YOU HAVE A DUSTPAN AND BRUSH, BROTHER.
THAT WAS TOO MUCH FUN...

OH, YAY! THE '*EVAPOR-TRANSPORTER-POD*' WORKED!
PING!
OH LOOK, EVIL EMPEROR PENGUIN HAS A PRETTY NEW OUTFIT.
OI! I'M HIS SISTER, RUTHLESS... *WHO ON EARTH ARE YOU?!*

OH, THAT DOESN'T BODE WELL...
WHAT?! WHAT ELSE COULD POSSIBLY GO WR...

...IT'S EVIL CAT, ISN'T IT.

I WANT TO SAY NO...

OOOH, YOU'RE ***CUTE!***
CAN I HAVE ONE?!
HE'S NOT FOR SALE. NOW, WHERE'S YOUR BROTHER? I'M HERE TO CONQUER HIM.
HEE HEE, THAT TICKLES!

I'M ***HERE!***
BANG
AND I'M ANGRY!

OH, HOLD ME WHILST I SHUDDER WITH FEAR.
EVIL CAT, WHAT DO YOU WANT NOW?!
YOU'RE A FUN KITTY CAT.

I DID COME FOR YOU, BUT I THINK I'LL TAKE YOUR SISTER INSTEAD... SHE COULD BE ***VERY*** USEFUL INDEED!
ZAP

GREAT... MUM'S GONNA KILL ME.

SIBLING RIVALRY: PART 2

PREVIOUSLY ON EEP...

EVIL CAT'S EVIL BASE

I'LL BE BACK TOMORROW.
YOU CAN'T JUST LEAVE ME IN HERE! HEY!

MY BROTHER WOULD NEVER COME LOOKING FOR ME. I RUINED ALL HIS EVIL STUFF.

ERR, HELLO, RUTH...
WOULD YOU LIKE A CUP OF TEA? OR ORANGE SQUASH, MAYBE?
GO AWAY! I WANT NOTHING TO DO WITH YOU HORRID CREATURES!

ERM, EVIL MASTER... DON'T YOU THINK WHAT YOU'RE DOING IS A LITTLE MEAN?
EUGENE...

I'M GOING TO PRETEND I DIDN'T HEAR WHAT YOU JUST SAID. NOW GET OUT BEFORE I TURN YOU INTO MARSHMALLOW ICE-CREAM!
YES, EVIL MASTER.

THAT NIGHT...

PSSSST!

I KNEW I COULD COUNT ON YOU, MR BUZZINGTON. HERE'S A TINY SCARF. IT'S COLD WHERE YOU'RE GOING...
Bzzzz
Bzzzzz

Bzzz
HEAVY...
Bzzz

BE SAFE, MR BUZZINGTON!
Bzzz

ANTARCTICA: EEP'S HQ
GAAAAAH! GET IT OUT! IT'S GOING TO STING ME! I SEE DEATH IN IT'S EYES!
SIR, IT'S JUST A TINY BEE... WAIT... LOOK, IT'S HOLDING SOMETHING.

IT'S AN ENVELOPE.
BRRzzzz
BRRzzzz

Dear Number 8,
Don't show this to EEP
He won't trust it...
Ruth is locked
away, I can help
you save her.
Use co-ordinates
3,19,81,2 to
find Evil Cat's base.
from ? x
P.S. I miss
you.

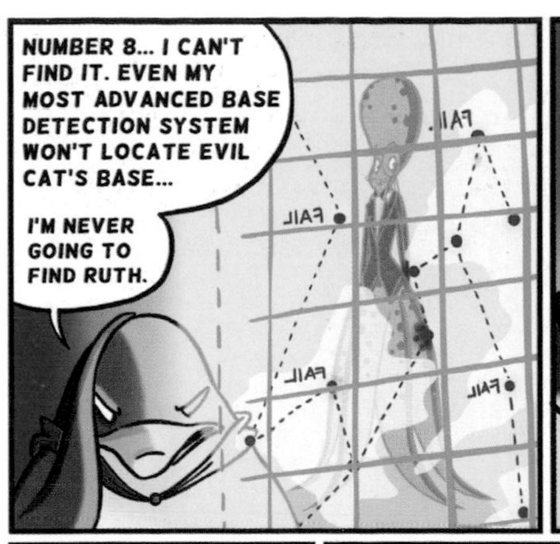
NUMBER 8... I CAN'T FIND IT. EVEN MY MOST ADVANCED BASE DETECTION SYSTEM WON'T LOCATE EVIL CAT'S BASE...
I'M NEVER GOING TO FIND RUTH.
FAIL
FAIL
FAIL
FAIL

WE HAVE TO FIND HER! IF MY MOTHER FINDS OUT, I'M TOAST! AND 'TOAST' IS A GENTLE WAY OF PUTTING IT...

HAVE YOU TRIED CO-ORDINATES, OH, I DON'T KNOW... SAAAAAY 3, 19, 81 AAAAND OH, LET'S SAY, NUMBER 2?!

LOCATION FOUND
SUCCESS

NUMBER 8! THAT'S IT! YOU'RE A GENIUS!

WELL, I WOULDN'T GO THAT FAR, SIR...
FINE, I WON'T. YOU NOT-QUITE-GENIUS. NOW, PREPARE THE FLYING POD OF EVIL!

CO-ORDINATES SET. LET'S GO GET RUTH! NO ONE MESSES WITH EVIL EMPEROR PENGUIN'S FAMILY!

MEANWHILE...
PSSSST. RUTH!
DIDN'T I TELL YOU TO LEAVE ME ALONE?

CLUNK

YOU HAVE TO FOLLOW ME, RUTH. QUICK!
THIS'LL BE YOUR ONLY CHANCE TO ESCAPE!

BUT WHY ARE YOU HELPING ME?!
YOU REMIND ME OF SOMEONE I USED TO KNOW... NOW, HURRY!
THIS WAY!

IT'S THAT BLASTED BEE AGAIN! I TOLD YOU, IT WANTS MY BLOOD!
SPLAT

NO, WAIT! OPEN THE SHIELD... QUICK!

PAH!
NO WAY! DON'T BE SO PREPOSTEROUS, NUMBER 8! AND TO THINK I CALLED YOU A GENIUS!

NUMBER 8. Ruth will be waiting at the top of the top hat... HURRY!

GOOD LUCK, RUTH. I MUST GO NOW BEFORE EVIL CAT NOTICES I'M GONE.
THANK YOU, EUGENE.

THERE SHE IS! THAT'S RUTH!
BROTHER!

QUICK, IN HERE!
HOW ON EARTH DID YOU MANAGE TO ESCAPE FROM EVIL CAT?!

THE CUTE LITTLE WHITE FLUFFY GUY HELPED ME... EUGENE WAS HIS NAME.
EUGENE?
HE WAS REALLY NICE.

YEAH. HE'S CERTAINLY NOT LIKE EVIL CAT.

OH YIPPEE!
WE DID IT, MR BUZZINGTON. RUTH IS SAFE NOW.

THE NEXT DAY...
WELL, BROTHER. I CAN'T SAY I'VE ENJOYED MY TIME HERE VERY MUCH. SO I'M GONNA GO BACK HOME.

AND YOUR SECRET IS SAFE WITH ME... THE BEING EVIL THING.
YOU'RE NOT VERY GOOD AT IT. I STILL THINK I COULD DO BETTER!

I'M SURE I'LL BE BACK TO DESTROY MORE OF YOUR EVIL STUFF. SO LONG!
WE'LL SEE ABOUT THAT... ...RUTH-LESS.

EVIL CAT'S EVIL BASE...
OKAY, LITTLE PENGUIN LADY, TIME TO-
WOH... WHAT?!
SHE'S... GONE?!

NOOOOO!!!
I WILL HAVE MY REVENGE, EVIL EMPEROR PENGUIN!

THE RETURN: PART 1

WHOOOOPS!
SMASH!!!
OH, DEARY DEAR.
HUH...?
OH MY! A HAPPY BLOB?! I'VE ALWAYS WANTED A HAPPY BLOB.
HEE HEE... I'M GOING TO KEEP YOU.
WHO'D HAVE THOUGHT YOU WERE THE PRODUCT OF A MIXTURE OF ULTIMATE EVIL...
THAT'S STRANGE...
I SWEAR YOU WERE SMALLER THAN THAT A SECOND AGO.
ERM... MR BLOB... YOU CAN STOP NOW.
EUGENE!
YOUR HOUR IS UP!
OH NO!

SO, WHERE IS IT?
THE ULTIMATE EVIL INVENTION THAT WILL ELIMINATE EVIL EMPEROR PENGUIN ONCE AND FOR ALL!

I JUST NEED A FEW MORE MINUTES, EVIL MASTER...
CUPBOARD OF DOOM
DO NOT ENTER
THERE ARE A COUPLE OF, ERR... MINOR TWEAKS I NEED TO MAKE.

THAT'S NOT GOOD ENOUGH! I SPECIFICALLY SAID, ONE HOUR!
CREEEAAK
AND WHY IS EVERYTHING SMASHED?!

AND WHY ARE YOU DRIPPING WITH... GOOEY STUFF?
GULP

ERM... THE CEILING IS, ERM, L-LEAKING...

EUGENE.
TELL ME WHAT'S GOING ON...

CREEEAK
BULGE
RIGHT NOW?!
WOBBLE

BOOM

EUGENE... WHAT IS THAT?
NO... NO. DON'T ANSWER THAT.

I'VE HAD ENOUGH OF THIS...
I WANT YOU TO LEAVE THE PREMISES, RIGHT NOW.
BUT, EVIL MASTER...

YOU'RE FIRED!!!

AND THAT MEANS YOU WON'T BE NEEDING THIS HAT...
NOW... GO.

THE RETURN: PART 2

PREVIOUSLY ON EEP...

TWO WEEKS LATER...

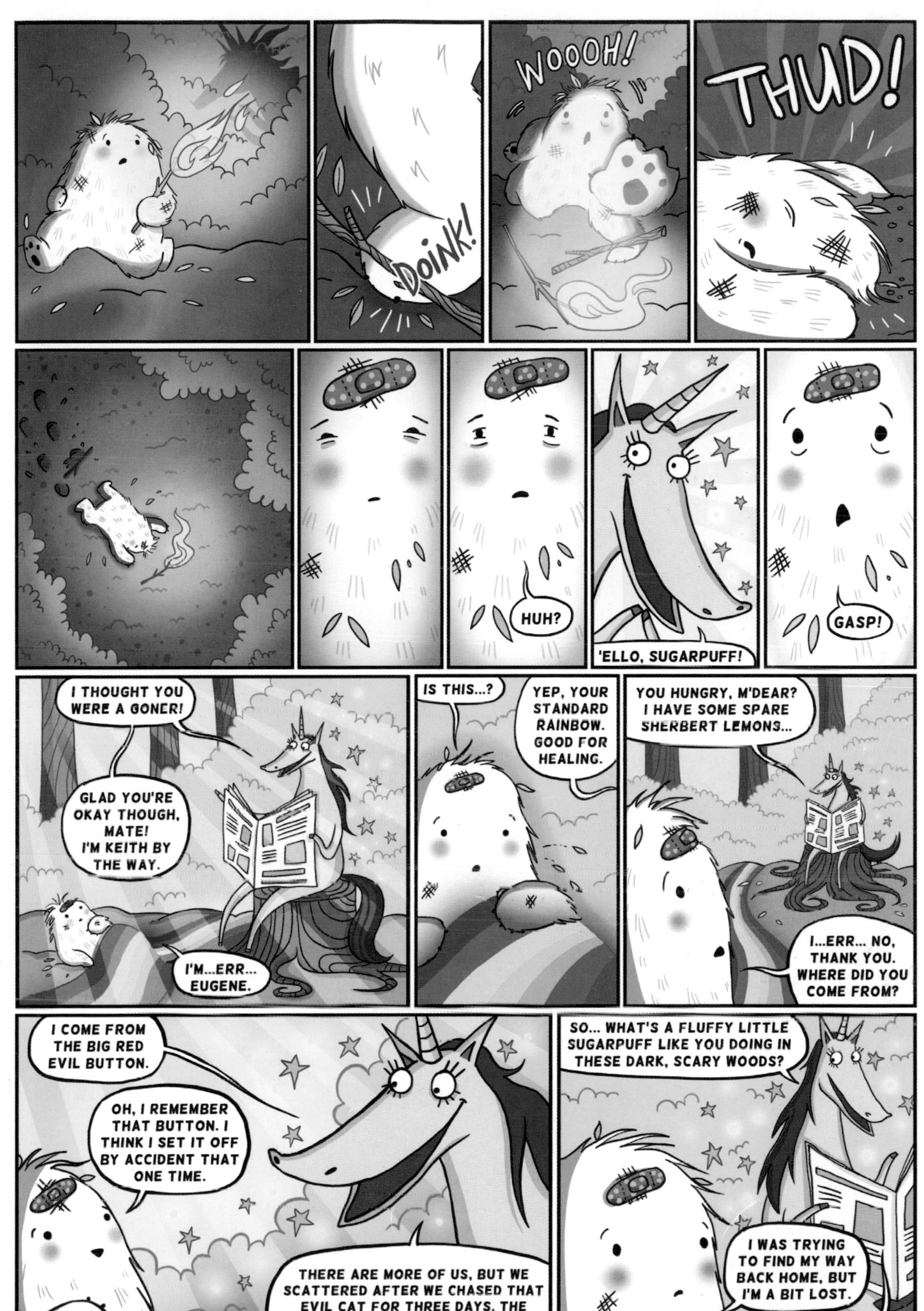
WOOOH!
DOINK!
THUD!
HUH?
'ELLO, SUGARPUFF!
GASP!
I THOUGHT YOU WERE A GONER!
GLAD YOU'RE OKAY THOUGH, MATE! I'M KEITH BY THE WAY.
I'M...ERR... EUGENE.
IS THIS...?
YEP, YOUR STANDARD RAINBOW. GOOD FOR HEALING.
YOU HUNGRY, M'DEAR? I HAVE SOME SPARE SHERBERT LEMONS...
I...ERR... NO, THANK YOU. WHERE DID YOU COME FROM?
I COME FROM THE BIG RED EVIL BUTTON.
OH, I REMEMBER THAT BUTTON. I THINK I SET IT OFF BY ACCIDENT THAT ONE TIME.
THERE ARE MORE OF US, BUT WE SCATTERED AFTER WE CHASED THAT EVIL CAT FOR THREE DAYS. THE HERD GET TOGETHER ONCE A MONTH TO DISCUSS UNICORN POLITICS.
SO... WHAT'S A FLUFFY LITTLE SUGARPUFF LIKE YOU DOING IN THESE DARK, SCARY WOODS?
I WAS TRYING TO FIND MY WAY BACK HOME, BUT I'M A BIT LOST.
WHERE'S HOME?

WHERE IT'S ALWAYS BEEN...
ANTARCTICA!
RUDDY COLD THERE... BUT HOME IS HOME, EH!
SOUNDS LIKE YOU'RE GONNA NEED A RIDE. LUCKY FOR YOU, I'M WELL UP FOR AN ADVENTURE RIGHT NOW!
YOU CAN FLY?!
WELL, I GUESS WE CAN CLASS IT AS FLYING...
OH, KEITH! YOU'RE THE BEST UNICORN I'VE EVER MET *EVER!*
YOU'RE THE ONLY UNICORN I'VE EVER MET... EVER.
BUT THAT'S OKAY, BECAUSE YOU'RE THE *BESTEST!*
OKAY, SUGAR-PUFF. HOP ON! LET'S GET YOU HOME.
NOW, HOLD ON TIGHT, OKAY!
ALRIGHTY. LET'S GO!
OH, KEITH, YOU'RE SO SOFT!
WHOOOOSH!
TO ANTARCTICA!!!

THE RETURN: PART 3

PREVIOUSLY ON EEP...

THIS GUY...

MET THIS GUY...

AND TOGETHER THEY'RE OFF TO...

ANTARCTICA!

HOURS LATER...

OOO, A DOUBLE RAINBOW!

THAT, MY FRIEND, IS WHAT THEY CALL GOOD LUCK!

YOU SHOULD MAKE A WISH... QUICK!

OH, YAY, I DID IT!

WHAA...

I HAD A FEELING YOU'D BE RUNNING BACK TO SERVE THAT PATHETIC LITTLE PENGUIN.

NAY!
WELL, NOT ON MY WATCH!
YOU MIGHT NOT BE *MY* MINION ANY MORE, BUT YOU CAN STILL BE MY *PRISONER*!!!

HOLD ON, EUGENE! I'VE GOT YOU!

HOW ABOUT YOU GIVE ME THE MINION BACK, *HORSE!*

OH NO HE DI'N'T...

I'M SLIPPING!
RAINBOW BLAST!

ACK! NO!
I WILL NOT BE BEATEN BY ONE MEASLY SPARKLE HORSE!

OH, THAT'S OKAY, YOU DON'T HAVE TO WORRY ABOUT ME...

WHEN THERE ARE *THIRTY SEVEN* MORE SPARKLY HORSES ON THEIR WAY!

PLING!
SMALL RED EVIL BUTTON

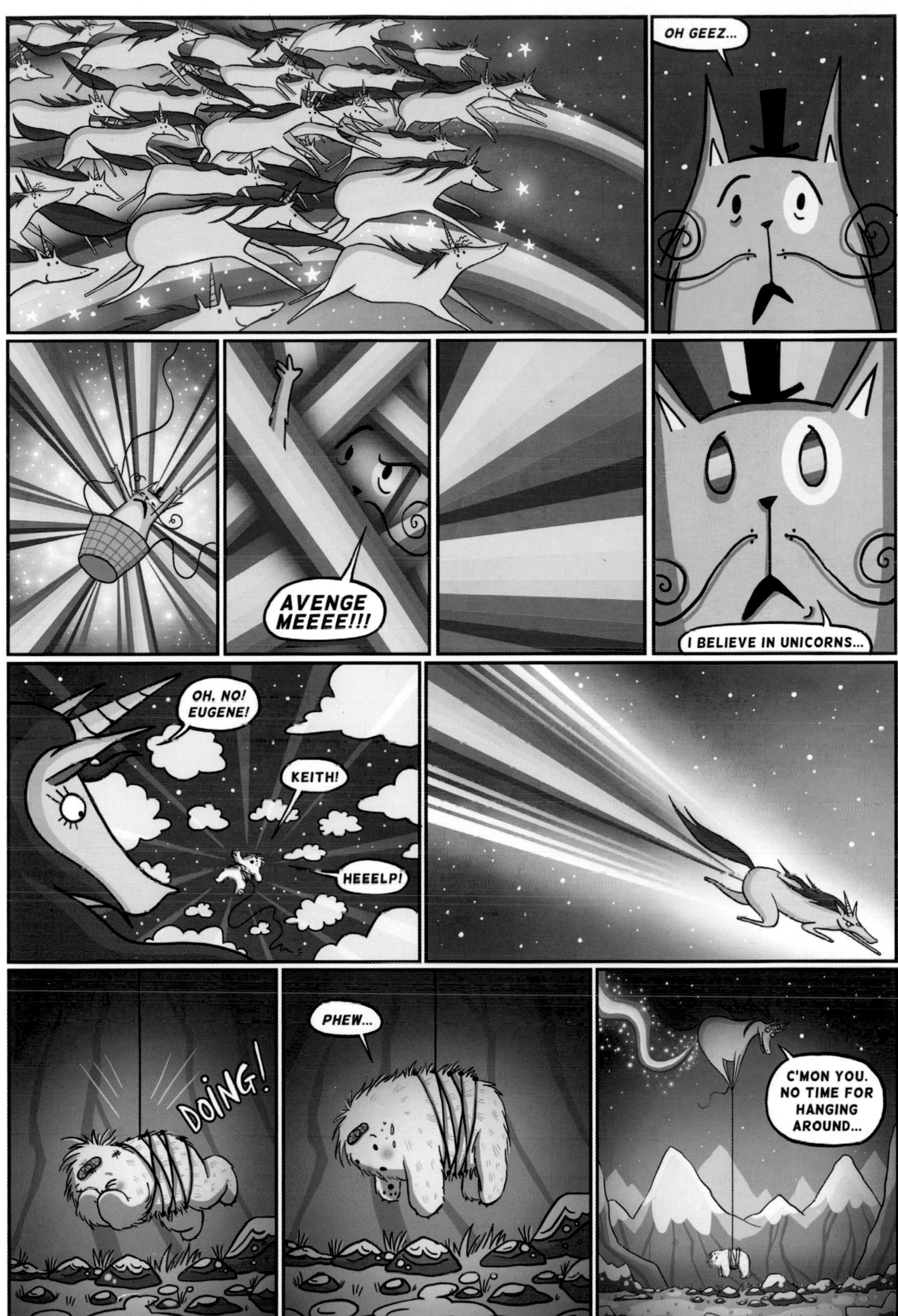
OH GEEZ...
AVENGE MEEEE!!!
I BELIEVE IN UNICORNS...
OH, NO! EUGENE!
KEITH!
HEEELP!
DOING!
PHEW...
C'MON YOU. NO TIME FOR HANGING AROUND...

THE RETURN: PART 4

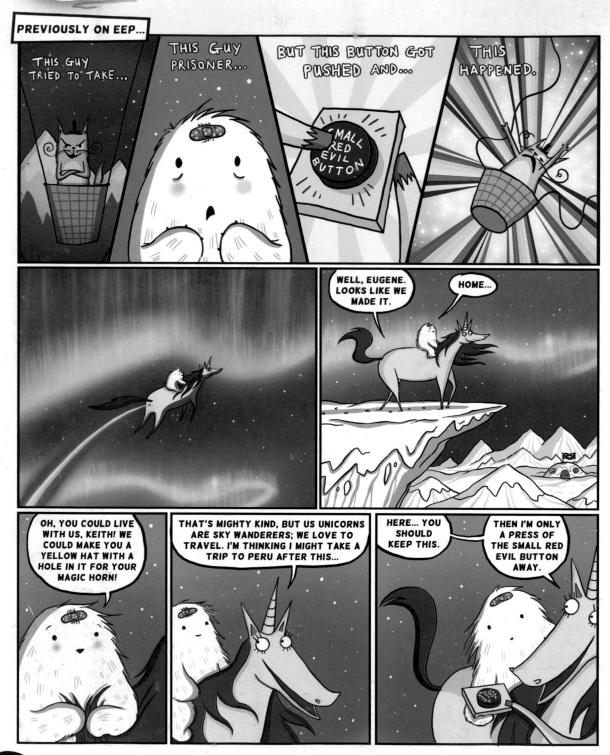

PREVIOUSLY ON EEP...

HERE... YOU SHOULD KEEP THIS.

THEN I'M ONLY A PRESS OF THE SMALL RED EVIL BUTTON AWAY.